BREAKFAST
AND OTHER JOURNEYS WE TAKE
David Payne

Copyright

Breakfast and Other Journeys We Take

All stories written by David Payne

Cover by David Payne, Photo by Kelly GravesonPayne

Copyright © 2024

Table of Contents

Content Warnings..1

Forward 3

Dedication 5

Flash 7

Precipice 11

Blood on the Wall..21

Chicks 31

Ocean Adventure..41

Hope...51

Pieces 61

Breakfast 67

Cat Discussion 71

About the Author...79

Content Warnings

"Flash" deals with themes of parental loss.

"Precipice" has suicide as a driver of the story.

"Blood on the Wall" has a main character struggling with dementia.

"Pieces" has divorce and a father trying to figure out what he can do to fix the relationship with his son.

As with any story, you might read more into the story than I intend or even thought about. If a story is making you uncomfortable, please do step away from it if it gets too much. If you are okay with the uncomfortableness, please continue.

Be mindful.

Forward

Thank you for picking up this book. Now if you could just buy it, that would make my day.

Let's start over.

All of the stories captured here deal with real life, most of them drawn heavily from my own experiences. I would not call them creative non-fiction, since they aren't retellings of those experiences, but there are similarities that I can't help but point out. In that sense, there is a fair bit of raw emotion in these stories that don't feature in some of my other works.

There's something about a regular thing we do, like breakfast, and thinking about it as an epic journey that strikes me as important. If I can get through each day and think about each little thing I did as a journey, I think I'm a happier person as a result. That's what this collection is trying to do. Get you out of your comfort zone, go on the journey. Not all of the journeys are going to be happy or fun, but they are worth taking if that's where you are.

I'm curious what others will take out of reading these stories, so if you are inclined to share, please take the time to leave a review, a rating. Or if you don't want it posted publicly, you are welcome to send me comments to my email (in the bio at the back of the book).

Thanks again for picking up the book. Now, let's embark on a journey. Together.

Dedication

This collection wouldn't be here without the persistent nagging of those in my chat from day to day. The support of my partner, Green Bean. The support of my children who make me laugh, cry, feel every day. It's been a journey to get here and I'm looking forward to the next one on the horizon. Thanks for all the support.

For those who know, this is where you hear me say: "Buy my book!" Thanks for laughing with me. (Bok bok bok)

To Nix: Thanks for hanging out with me. They promised to buy five copies if I leave this statement in here.

Flash

I stood at the window and my mother had just gotten into her car - an old Ford Escort wagon with a replaced axle and a clutch that was on its way out - when the lightning struck. As far as I can remember, there was no space between the lightning and the thunder. I remember getting up from the floor and feeling like the whole world had lost color. I couldn't hear anything as I got to my feet, and the air crackled around me. The little hairs on my arm stood out straight.

Outside, my mother's car was there, but it was raining so hard, I couldn't make out what was going on in there. I think I wanted to run out and make sure she was okay, but something held me back. Someone? Right, my father was there, holding me tight.

The ringing in my ears started, intensified, and then as it died down, I could hear other things. The rumble of thunder, the rain pattering, my father saying to stay put. Lightning struck again, bright flashes that made my flinch into my father so hard that he had trouble keeping a hold of me.

"She'll be okay. Better in the car than in the rain. She'll be fine."

I looked up, and his eyes were fixed on the car out there. His hands were tight on my shoulders, but his focus was outside. More crashes of lightning. More thunder. Rain constant and thicker than it should have been.

"She'll be fine. She's alright. Just stay in the car. Don't move." He kept repeating the words and I got the impression it wasn't for me.

I twisted out of his grip, which wasn't as firm on me as I had thought. His hands just dropped to his side, like he barely remembered I was there. His eyes were still locked on the car.

It was morning, and while we didn't need the lights on anymore, they had been on before the strike. "Is the power out?" I asked. I walked into the kitchen to look at the microwave and as I suspected, the clock was black. "Power's out."

"We'll be fine. Summer storms are not so bad."

I stopped counting the lightning and thunder, it was just too frequent. I knew the wind was bad out there too, but how could I pay attention to that when the rain was just a solid wall against our windows? The faint forms of the trees at the far side of the driveway swaying dangerously wide reminded me of the wind. I couldn't even hear the wind with how heavy the rain was, but it was there.

A sharp crack jolted my attention, but this wasn't thunder. No, this was a tree that ripped apart and fell across the back driveway. "Mom needs to get back inside. Storm's getting worse."

"No. She's safe out there. As long as she's in the car, she'll be fine."

"Dad! A tree just broke out there. If one falls on the car, she'll be dead!" I headed for the door and wrenched it open. The thin metal door with glass panes seemed like such a bad idea for an outer door. I expected my father to stop me, but either I had moved too fast or he really did agree with me. I put my hand on the handle, and the storm drifted away, like it was barely more than a memory.

The rain-soaked ground ran little rivers everywhere. Branches fallen. Trees rent. And my mother's car was there, crushed under not one but three different trees. Only it wasn't her car - not that red Ford Escort wagon with the new axle and the bad clutch. No this was rusted and broken, only faint flecks of faded paint anywhere. It had been there for so long.

"Where'd the storm go?" I asked, looking over to my father, but he wasn't there either. He was long gone. They were both gone, I remembered. The storm had been so long ago. This was my house. Or the memory of it, because it wasn't mine any more. The power was out. Same now as then.

The power is out.

I open the door, and step out, careful on the broken poured concrete steps that my father had set up in the 70s. They are cracked, broken, and perilous now, time and weather doing what they did. Wearing things down. Eroding and destroying.

"Why am I here?" I ask, trying to shake some sense into my head. This isn't my house anymore. That house was lost, destroyed in the storm, along with everything else. The car, my family. My brothers. They are all gone.

The rain-soaked ground becomes storm tossed debris and detritus. The rusted and destroyed car becomes dust, and the trees that held it down cut and removed. Now that I am outside and looking back at that house - white shingles, faded with age and sun - roof caved in, eaves broken off. Windows gone. Even the outer door - metal and glass - broken off its hinges. Lay on the ground like it had always been there. Or at least, had always been there since the storm.

I walk the path away from the house, to the driveway where another car waits. Blue. Sedan. Mine, I thought. I think.

The intersection of past and present are unsettling. Why am I here? I don't ask it out loud. There's no one here anyway.

The house behind me is crushed. I look at it, seeing it both as it is - a destroyed husk - and as it was - a beautiful place where I grew up. I clench my hand into a fist as I feel that frustration from a lack of control, and a paper crumples up in my hand. I bring it up, read the heading. It's a deed. The deed. For this place. It haunts me.

But it is mine again. Time to rebuild.

Precipice

Dan stood on the edge of Lover's Leap, a rock formation overlooking Purgatory Chasm below. He had stood there so many times, he mused that you could see his footprints worn into the rock over the years. It was his favorite place to stand, looking down on the hikers that made their way through the short chasm. His chasm, in his mind. He grew up hiking through it, and when he was a teenager, it was where he would take his girlfriend when they wanted some alone time. Even though it was a public area, there were many ill-used trails that they could get lost in.

He enjoyed hiking a lot, and while this particular hike was too short for most serious hikers, it offered some nice variety and was very close to home. He could run over to it on a good day, and frequently did, since parking was sometimes at a premium. Dan had run over on this day, leaving his phone at home because he didn't want to be disturbed, not even taking a canteen with him for the run. He didn't want those burdens with him, dragging him down.

This particular spring day, Dan stood up on his rock overlooking his chasm, wondering what had brought him there that day. He had been down on his luck, down on his life, down on those around him. Depressed was too easy a word for it, though he supposed that's what he was. He came out to the chasm when he needed to be picked up, to be encouraged. And often he was. It had a raw, natural beauty about it, despite the hundreds of people who crowded through it day after day. In the spring, the crowds were usually pretty heavy as long as the snow had enough time to melt away, but it was early enough in the spring that they hadn't. Also, the day before had seen plenty of rain, so he trudged through the mud to his favorite spot. And he stood and looked out and down. Right then, there were only two hikers below. The type of intrepid souls who, like himself, preferred the chasm when there weren't heavy crowds no doubt.

Up at the top of the chasm, it was chilly, and there was a stiff wind that blew through the trees, that made it seem more so. With so much moisture from the previous day's rains, it felt like the air was made of water. It was the kind of weather that made the woods smell like the woods. And he loved that. Dan knew the crisp air would be cooler down in the chasm proper.

Standing there, on his rock, he wondered who had first fallen from it. It was called Lover's Leap after all, and he supposed it was less likely to be innocently named, but he hadn't really looked into it. The whole of the chasm had all kinds of references to death, hell, and it was, of course, named Purgatory. Still, it was such a peaceful place to him. Over the years, he suspected there were a lot who had considered suicide here, and he wondered why he never heard about it. Why he never saw any indication of it? He shrugged. It was a gloomy, morbid idea, but that was the kind of mood he ws in.

A bird, an oriole, flew overhead and landed on a branch not too far away from him. He watched it for a moment, as it, in turn, eyed him, and whatever else it fancied around. It observed, and then it flew off. Dan tracked it until he lost sight of it. Then he was back to his own thoughts. He decided it wasn't good to be in his own thoughts.

DAN TOOK A SEAT, HIS legs dangling over the edge. To some, that would be too much, too dangerous. To Dan, this was comfortable. Home even. This was where he belonged.

There was the rustle of leaves behind him. Some other hiker on this oft-forgotten trail. Sometimes, he was the only one who traveled the trail the whole of the day. This person came up the trail on their own, and didn't stop to look out over the rock, like Dan had. They just passed by and Dan was left alone again.

What was he doing up here? Why did he find himself at this place? What drew him here?

He knew of course. When things were not going well, Dan sought out the things that made Dan, Dan. And things were not going well for Dan. He hoped the rocks of the chasm had better answers. It seemed unlikely though.

Dan wasn't watching the time, wasn't really sure how long he'd been up there, on the rock, standing, then sitting, legs hanging out over the edge. Somehow, the sun was close to setting, which meant that the park would be closed soon and he would have to leave. He didn't bring his car, and he could walk home in the dark, even through the woods. That was nothing new to him. And for some reason, he didn't want to leave his rock. It was more home than home was.

AS DARKNESS SETTLED in, he heard rustling leaves behind him again. It was too late for another hiker, and the movement headed away from the parking lot, so that seemed even less likely. He turned and saw, not twenty feet away, a black bear emerging from the underbrush. Dan had faced bears before, and the black bears around the chasm were usually timid enough that they would scamper at any sign of human activity. But this was close to night, and Dan knew that he didn't want to face a bear of any size when there was no one else around. He turned fully around, swinging his legs up onto the rock, and wondered what his best course was. There was a path down into the chasm from the side of the rock. It was precarious at best during the day time. At night, he imagined it was near impossible without a rope. Alternatively, he would have to find a way around the bear. Or find a way to scare it off.

The bear had clearly noticed him, and since he wasn't doing much, it wasn't approaching or moving away at any special speed. They just watched each other. Dan fought to keep his breathing even, regular. And the presence of the bear kept his mind off of the other things that were bothering him. In a way, this was the most liberated he felt in quite some time.

The bear rooted around at the ground for a bit, clearing some leaves away. *Looking for something to eat probably*, Dan thought. He considered the path down into the chasm again. It was the only way he could go that didn't involve getting closer to the bear. And even though he felt it was likely the bear would back off if he showed it his full size and tried to stand even taller, the reality was he wouldn't really have a backup plan if that failed. His back was to a seventy foot drop or more, and he wouldn't be able to navigate the path down if he had to run at all.

He edged down the rock towards the path, reasoning it was his best option out of several bad ones. The rock was slick with the early evening air, damp as it was to begin with. He could feel the wetness seep into his clothing, stinging him in places because it was cold. Why had he stayed out so long? It all seemed so foolish now.

THE BEAR CAME CLOSER, keeping him in sight as he descended the side of the rock, half-sliding, half-crawling down. It was much darker out than he realized, and as he looked down below him, to make sure he wasn't going to just go off the edge, he took his eyes off the bear for a moment. And when he looked back, he realized he had lost track of it. Panicking a little more, he concentrated on getting down. Wherever the bear was, if he could get down off of the rock and into the chasm, he could get his way out without further trouble. He hoped.

Dan left his phone back at home. He hadn't wanted to be disturbed while he was out. Now that looked like a horrible idea. He wished he had brought something.

His heel caught on the rock suddenly, propelling him in a way he wasn't expecting. As he crawled to a stop, his fingers wrapped around the edge of the rock. The edge of the rock, off of which he almost fell. He realized he was breathing hard, nearly hyperventilating. Calm yourself, he thought. Slow your breaths. Take deliberate movements.

He pulled himself away from the edge again, found where the edge of the rock met the path. There was a thin tree there. He remembered that. It was what he could use to swing down to the next ledge. But he wouldn't be able to see that ledge. He would be swinging onto it blindly. With a bear possibly very close by.

He chanced a look back up, but still couldn't see the bear. Couldn't hear it either, at least, but not knowing where it was was so much worse than being sure of where it was. Why hadn't he brought a light with him at least? His phone would have solved that. He chided himself again, but stamped down that feeling. He had to concentrate. He had to find a way down. He clambered down, found where he usually held the tree's trunk, and swung out tentatively. He barely touched the far ledge with his toes as he swung. So he had a better than rough idea of where he needed to swing to. Swinging back, he landed and then swung out again, with more force, and let go, in his best confidence.

For half a moment, he thought he had missed completely, but then his foot made contact with the ledge awkwardly. As he set more weight on it, his foot slipped, his leg buckled, and he came crashing down onto his knees. Pain shot through his knees as he hit the rock with full force, slamming his palms onto the rock to save his face. Pain came from everywhere. He knew he must be bleeding now. He sat back, his back against the rock face, and wondered where the bear was. It was darker down in the chasm, darker than it had already been at the top. Was this really his best course? He wondered if he was going to make it out alive.

HE WRUNG HIS HANDS together, rubbing off the grit from the stone and feeling sharp pains as he did so from where he had flayed his own skin. From the ledge, he should have been able to make his way down. He knew it did some switchbacks along the way, but he was hopefully only about ten feet up now. He thought.

Standing up, he bumped his head on the rock above, remembering too late that he had to hunch over on this part. He didn't hit hard, but even hitting one's head softly against an unseen rock still hurt. It didn't help him remain focused. He held his throbbing head with one hand, guided his path along with his right hand, and slowly stepped one foot forward at a time. One step. Then another. Then a third. As he took his fourth, his foot went off the ledge. *Right. There was the switchback*, he thought. He felt around and found the way down from there, taking one cautious step at a time. Three, four. Then air again, switchback. And before long, he found himself standing on the chasm floor. Mentally, he could picture what he had to cross in order to get out of the chasm. He knew the path through the chasm very well, but with it so dark in the chasm, he had little mental reference to any of it.

As he collected himself, he thought he heard a noise, so he stood stock still. The hair on the back of his neck stood up and he swore he felt warm air on the back of his neck. He whirled around, lashing out with his arms, and they collided with the rocks he had just climbed down. Pain ran through his arms, and he immediately regretted it. He clutched his hands as they throbbed, stumbling away from the rock face, trying to picture where he was in the chasm after so many trips through it. He stepped cautiously, feeling his way along with his feet, but each step sent pain through his knees. Every step he took was an exercise, and in his panicked mind, he was making no headway, and the bear might as well have been upon him. He wondered again whether it had even followed him down, but he couldn't worry about it. He had to focus on getting out of the chasm. Nothing else mattered until he did that.

He kicked softly into a rock that jutted upward. He remembered this part. Dan put his hands out and felt the shape of the rock, pictured where in the chasm it was and how he should go around it. *To the right. Then a step up between it and the next rock*, he thought. Then brace his hands against the large rock to the right, and step carefully because there were gaps between the rocks here. It was a common place for people to twist ankles, he knew the gaps well. Each step seemed to take a lifetime, and he felt like progress was taken in inches, if at all.

He stepped around the gaps and felt soft, squishy earth beneath his feet. *This was right*, he thought. He breathed a little easier. He was closer to the exit now, *just three more... no four more rocks to navigate around*. And then the steep final climb up. It was only up to his shoulders, and it was easy to manage in the light. He wasn't sure it would be so simple in the dark though.

Dan found the next rock to go around easily, and after he was passed the one gap near it, he realized there weren't any more gaps to navigate. Just rough, uneven ground with sharp rocks and unforgiving roots poking up. The next rock came soon after and he hefted himself up along side it, ducking down to avoid a branch that reached out over the rock, as he went around. And on to the next, and then the last one. He was so close now. So very close.

SUDDENLY, THERE WAS a rustling in the leaves. But there were no leaves down in the chasm that hadn't been crushed under so many feet. The noise came from nearby, above him. *The bear!* Had it followed him? He slipped on a rock, but caught himself before he fell. He scanned the darkness, seeing the silhouette of the skeletal trees above him against the dark night sky. He didn't see any signs of movement, but there was still some rustling up there. Dan didn't feel any wind on him, but he was in the a sheltered area of the chasm, so he suspected there wouldn't be any for him anyway. Still, the rustling sounded like movement, and the movement to him meant a bear stalking after him.

He tried to put the bear from his mind, even as his breath quickened, sweating despite the chill in the air. Dan ran his injured hands along the rock face. He just needed to find the last few steps up, and then he would just have a few hundred feet to get to the road. He wondered why he couldn't see any lights. Surely the pavilion had them? But maybe they didn't stay on at night. That was possible. How late was it?

He shook his head. Concentrate, he thought. Get yourself out of here, worry about all that later. You're almost there.

Then he ran into the wall that he would need to climb over. It didn't hurt because he had been expecting it, and was going so slowly. The rocks were freezing cold now, but that might have been just for him. He realized his whole body was freezing, even in the places where he was likely bleeding. Dan wondered what a sight he would be if he caught himself in the mirror.

He pulled himself up the first half of the wall, planting his feet on a rock he remembered nearby. As he started to pull himself up the rest of the way though, a rock kicked down onto his hands. Not a big one, but big enough to hurt nonetheless. And it had come from above him. Panicking, he nearly pushed off and away from the rock, but that would have sent him sprawling to the ground.

He couldn't stop though, he needed to get up to get out. If the bear was there, he was so much worse below it. Fighting against his fears, he vaulted up, right into the warm breath of whatever was there. It was foul-smelling, horrible. He pictured it as a ravenous beast, ready to devour him, even though he knew intellectually that black bears rarely attacked humans. He reasoned it was just hungry, curious. But his instincts - they ruled over him. Everything about him on the inside wanted to cut and run. But he knew there were a lot of rocks between where he was and the road, so running was foolish.

Standing up as tall as he could, he faced toward the thing in the dark, raised his hands up high, and roared as loud as he could. And when he stopped, he couldn't feel anything before him. Nothing breathed on him and he didn't hear anything moving. Was anything there in the first place? He couldn't be sure.

Dan tried to put it out of his mind. His heart still raced. His breath was still short. But he stepped one cautious step after another until he reached the pavilion. He sat down on one of the benches there, catching his breath, wishing he could just be home. Once he had calmed, listening to the night sounds and being relieved that nothing was moving near him, he stood up, found his way to the road and then walked home. It took him half a mile to find the first street light to help guide his way.

Blood on the Wall

Arnaud felt the sweat bead up on his forehead. His gaze was affixed on the wall before him, transfixed, and unwavering, trying to understand what he saw, what he would do about what he saw. On the white wall before him, was the most clear and distinct hand print he had ever seen. The kind of thing you would see in a television show as the firm evidence to throw some criminal in the clink forever. And that's the kind of thing he was thinking about because this hand print was red.

Most likely blood, he had already decided, but couldn't come up with a way to test that without having a professional come along. His peculiar need to have things clean ached to wipe it clean, to get rid of all evidence of it, but that's what it was, evidence. He wasn't sure what it was evidence of though. Nothing good of course, but what exactly had happened?

Arnaud coughed a little, gagging on the thought of it being blood. Whose blood was it though? And what had happened?

Throughout the house - a single story ranch, with two bedrooms - there wasn't a single other sound traveling. Arnaud stepped away from the wall, his gaze still lingering on it as he moved, and then down to the floor when his foot slipped a little in something wet. He grimaced as his mind immediately assumed the worst. Assumed that this was more evidence that someone would have to deal with.

Arnaud looked down, and sure enough, there was more of the blood - and now he was certain of its nature. Here it was a particularly heavy puddle of it, pooled in place because of the uneven nature of the floor into a rough oval. His foot sat in the middle of the puddle, the blood sloshing up around his foot like water, only this left him feeling nauseous immediately.

Arnaud pulled his foot out of the puddle, but hung it in the air. He stepped carefully on his heel, and paid attention to the floor as he stepped awkwardly through the house to the bathroom. He stepped into the tub, turned on the faucet, and let the water wash over his bare foot, blood sending streaks through the water toward the drain. He let the water run that way for a while, until all signs of the blood were gone. And then he let it run some more too.

The whole time he stood there in the tub, his mind raced, thought about what he should do, what had happened, what he should do. What should he do?

He turned off the water, stepped out of the tub and dried off his feet on the bath mat. He stared out at the hallway, or at least the section of it he could see from the bathroom and willed it to be clean of all the blood. To not have any more signs of whatever atrocities had been committed. He knew he should call the police. But what would that accomplish really, until he knew what was going on? He didn't want to go back out into the hallway and see it, but he couldn't just hide in the bathroom for the rest of his life either. He resolved he should call the police, and stepped out, watching carefully where he stepped and at the same time, avoiding looking at the conspicuous puddles in his home.

Arnaud made it to the kitchen, where he had set down his phone on the table when he had come in. Arnaud picked it up and dialed the emergency line. After a moment, there was a response on the other end.

"NINE-ONE-ONE. WHAT'S your emergency?" The voice sounded like it was coming through a tin can. It was a woman's voice he decided, but not anyone he recognized.

"Ummm. I don't actually know. I just got home and there's blood on my wall and on the floor."

"Is someone hurt sir?"

"I assume so, but I live alone, and I don't see anyone here. I haven't looked through the whole house though." Arnaud wondered if he should have investigated further before calling. That seemed like a bad idea though if there was some sort of sinister force in his house.

"Is someone hurt?"

"I don't know. I'm not hurt. Please send someone."

"Police and ambulance are already dispatched sir. Please stay on the line with me. Tell me what you saw."

"Well, there's a bloody hand print on my wall," he started, dreading the memory of it and wishing he could clean it off. "And there's a puddle of blood on the floor near it. There might be more. I stepped in the puddle, I didn't see it until then."

"Okay sir. Stay where you are now. Do you hear anyone in the house with you?"

"No. No one else is here. I live alone."

"Okay good. Stay on the line with me until the police get there. Is the door unlocked?"

"Yes. Well, the back door is. I never use the front door."

"Okay, I'll send them to the back then. One moment please, sir."

Arnaud could hear the woman talking to someone else. Dispatching directions he guessed. He could hear some sirens coming closer, though they were still far away. He felt the need to clean his house. He looked around the kitchen, wishing he had done the dishes before he left in the morning He stepped around through the kitchen, putting dishes into the sink so he could wash them. Or at least, put them into the dishwasher that he never used. He just couldn't leave them alone.

"What are you doing sir?" the voice of the woman said, coming back on the line.

"The dishes. I need to clean a little if there's going to be people in here."

"Don't touch anything sir. Please wait for the police to arrive."

Arnaud stopped, but his hands couldn't handle standing there. He just couldn't manage to leave it alone. "What if I just do these dishes? I just left these out this morning, and it would be horrible for anyone to come in with them out here."

"I can't let you do that. The police will be there in just a moment. Can you hear the sirens?"

"I can. They are getting closer."

"Good. Please stay where you are to receive them. The door is unlocked?"

"Yes. I said that already."

"Indeed you did. I'm just here to keep you talking sir."

"Okay. I'm here. I'm not going anywhere."

ARNAUD COULD SEE THE flashing lights now. They stopped in front of his house. One cruiser. Two. Three. Four. There might have been more. Maybe one of them was an ambulance, though he wondered why one would come. He hadn't seen anything that would necessitate one. Well, other than the blood. But what were the chances there was still someone needing help after whatever had caused such a huge amount of blood to be left on his wall and on the floor?

A knock came to the door, but Arnaud didn't even have a moment to respond before it opened and behind it an officer stepped in.

"The police are here now. Should I hang up?"

"Yes sir. Thank you for calling. The police will handle things now." There was a click and the phone hung up. He set it down on the table and looked at the officer.

He was younger than Arnaud, maybe early thirties, and chiseled with hard features, a stern glare, and a severe hair cut that betrayed a scar on his forehead and skull. Arnaud wondered where a police officer would get such a scar, and wondered more why he would keep his hair cut short enough to feature it.

The officer was taking in the details of the kitchen, to Arnaud's discomfort. Arnaud fought the urge to throw the dishes into the dishwasher.

"The blood is in the other room. Over here," he started to say, but the officer held up a hand in front of him.

"Stay where you are sir. We'll take it from here."

"Sure." Arnaud pursed his lips. More uncomfortable than ever.

The officer stepped in through the door and was followed by others. More with concentrated looks and hard features. People Arnaud wouldn't want to meet in an alley, he decided. He was very uncomfortable with so many guns in the house.

The first two officers made their way into the house proper, barely acknowledging Arnaud. The third, and then the fourth and fifth came in and cornered Arnaud in the kitchen, standing by the sink with him. Two of them had little notebooks out, the third stood between them and started asking him questions.

"Your name sir?"

"Arnaud. Arnaud Grovers."

"You just get home Mr. Grovers?"

"Please Arnaud. Yes. I just got home. I dropped my keys and phone on the table there, and stopped when I first saw the blood on the wall. Then I didn't see the puddle on the floor and stepped in it. From there, I went to the bathroom to wash off my foot."

"Sure. Sure." The officer nodded like she understood, but didn't particularly care about the details. Arnaud couldn't help but feel like the officers weren't taking him seriously. He cleared his throat and the officer asking him questions looked him straight in the eyes.

"You live here alone, Arnaud?"

Arnaud nodded.

"And when you left there was no one here?"
"Right."
"Any signs of a break in?"

ARNAUD INSTINCTIVELY started to shake his head, but looked down at the door he had come through. Suddenly he wasn't sure if it was actually locked or, for that matter, closed when he came in. It must have been, he had closed it when he left, but the details were so foggy to him now. He looked back at the officer.

"I... I am not certain. I think my door was locked. I definitely used the key, but I'm not sure I tried the door before that."

"Sure." Arnaud realized that the other two officers were writing down everything he said. He craned his neck to look over at their notes, but they shifted away so he couldn't see. Arnaud frowned, frustrated.

There was a knock at the open door. Two EMTs came in, though they didn't bring a stretcher with them. They waited in the doorway expectantly. One of the officers called them over to Arnaud.

"Take Mr. Grovers here..."

"Arnaud, please."

"Right. Take Arnaud and have him checked out. Seems a bit in shock."

"From the dispatch there was talk of blood," one of the EMTs said.

"We'll get you if there's anything else."

The EMTs nodded and took Arnaud out the door. Arnaud looked back, wondering if he'd get back into his house or not. He found himself answering questions to the EMTs but without hearing the questions. Like someone else was in control of his body. He tried to focus. What had the officer said? Shock? That seemed likely. As Arnaud stepped outside he realized he didn't have his shoes or socks on. When had he taken them off? Even that detail wasn't clear.

The EMTs helped him into the ambulance and started checking out his vitals. Arnaud, for his part, let them do what they needed to do. Everything was just a little wrong. The more he tried to pinpoint the details of anything, the less anything fit together. It was like the whole of the night were shattered like glass hit by a baseball and he was only able to pick up one piece at a time. And each time he did, he would cut himself, and he'd be bleeding, and there was nothing he could do to stop it. Suddenly, his whole body felt like it was bleeding.

"Am I bleeding?" he asked, trying to not call attention to his own discomfort, but needing someone else to tell him he was okay. The EMT looked at him, a little concerned, and shook his head.

"Not as far as we can tell, Arnaud. Why, do you feel like you are bleeding?"

ARNAUD CONSIDERED THAT for a moment. Was he crazy? He shook his head. "No. I don't think so. Just wondering where all that blood came from."

"Didn't you tell 911 that it was on the wall and floor when you got there?"

"I did. And it was. I'm just... I'm just very confused right now. Nothing seems to be making sense."

This seemed to make sense to the EMT though and he tried to reassure Arnaud by putting his hand on his shoulder.

"We think you are in shock, sir. Keep lying down, and we'll see about clearing out the confusion and it should all come back in due time. For now, just relax."

There was some static over the EMT's walkie, and then Arnaud just barely caught the voice on the other end. "... keep Mr. Grovers in the ambulance. Do not let him go."

Arnaud couldn't be certain he had heard that correctly, but the EMT's body language changed appreciatively in that moment. Arnaud tried to sit up, "Why are they telling you to keep me in here?" he asked, panicking a little more and more.

"I don't know sir. For now, just lay back and rest. I'll see if I can get the details sorted out."

"I don't know if I can relax now. Really, what is going on?" Arnaud was still fighting with himself on what details were going on in his head, and what was actually happening.

"Just wait. Let me see if I can learn something. I'll just step out for a minute."

Arnaud did not lay back down, but didn't stop the EMT from exiting the ambulance. Once outside, the EMT said something into his walkie, and waited for a response. When it came, Arnaud didn't hear it. The EMT closed the door most of the way, and was apparently talking to the other EMT or one of the officers out there. Arnaud sat forward, trying to catch the conversation, but couldn't make out any of the words. He had an impulsive thought to try to escape the ambulance. If he did though, where would he go? He didn't even have his shoes on. And he was hungry. When was the last time he ate? He didn't have anything when he got home. So around lunch time maybe? It was a while. But the details were so fuzzy. Just like everything else.

"Excuse me," he called out tentatively. "Excuse me." He repeated it a little louder.

The EMT poked his head around the door. "Arnaud, do you know a Mr. Thurman?"

Arnaud looked at the EMT, puzzled. The name first seemed nonsense to him, then it became clearer. After a moment, he nodded. "Yes. He's... he's my nurse."

"Ok. Good. Glad you remember that. And what did Mr. Thurman give you for breakfast today?"

"Breakfast?" Arnaud thought about the word for a moment. Breakfast was so far away. He shook his head after a bit. "I... I don't remember. I'm sure I had something. I just don't remember what."

MR. THURMAN OPENED the door fully. "Toast with strawberry jelly, sir."

Arnaud looked at the stranger in the doorway, confused. "Toast, with strawberry jelly," he repeated, tasting it in his mouth, but it didn't seem like something he would have for breakfast.

"Come on Arnaud. Time to go home." Mr. Thurman coaxed him out of the ambulance. Arnaud followed the instructions, not really having a reason to deny them, and still being so very much confused about everything. Arnaud leaned forward and looked at his bare feet.

"How can I go home without shoes?" he asked.

"Arnaud, you don't have shoes. Come on. I'll help you back to your house."

"But I should have shoes, shouldn't I? Where did they go?" Arnaud didn't remember where he put them. Did he have them on when he came in?

Mr. Thurman offered a hand to Arnaud to help him out of the ambulance. Outside, the house looked much as it did before, including the half dozen police cruisers outside. The flashing lights were very distracting to Arnaud. He couldn't focus on anything, just swiveled his head from one set of lights to the next.

Mr. Thurman patted his arm affectionately. "There, there. Let's get you back inside."

Arnaud felt the cold of the ground on his feet. His shoes. He needed shoes.

The house was close now. Mr. Thurman kept pulling him closer. "Almost there. Come on now. We can get there."

"Mr. Thurman, where are my shoes? I had shoes didn't I?"

"You don't have shoes Arnaud. It's been years since you've gone outside."

"Years?" he asked, still more confused. "No, I just came back in when I called the police. There was blood on the wall. On the floor."

"No Arnaud. That was strawberry jelly. Not blood. It was from this morning."

Arnaud looked at Mr. Thurman critically. "What are you talking about?"

"Arnaud, you threw the toast at me this morning. You were having an episode and threw your toast. And then took a huge glob of it out of the jar and dropped it on the ground when I told you to clean it up."

Arnaud looked at Mr. Thurman like he was crazy. Arnaud didn't even like toast. And certainly not strawberry jelly. Why would he even have that?

Arnaud allowed himself to be taken inside. The police were clearing out, and looked at Arnaud sympathetically. Arnaud took it as pity though. They all thought he was crazy. He walked to the hallway and looked at the blood on the wall. He looked at the hand print.

"That was after you dropped that glob of jelly on the ground. You leaned against the wall." Mr. Thurman also had a pitying look on his face. How was this right to treat someone this way? He was outraged. But he wasn't exactly sure what he had done, or why everyone looked at him that way.

"Come on Arnaud. Time for bed."

"Wait," Arnaud said, leaning his hand against the wall over the hand print. It matched his hand. He put his finger in the jelly puddle on the ground and then put his finger in his mouth.

Weird, he thought.

Apparently strawberry jelly was tasty after all.

Chicks

"What exactly are we supposed to do with two hundred chicks?"

"We'll raise them, they'll give us eggs... what are we not supposed to do with them?"

Fran looked at her partner George with equal parts incredulity and horror. He had just returned from the market and in the back of the van was an enormous basket with a large number of chicks. As in baby chickens. As in hundreds of mouths to feed. As in things that would need a place to stay, be cared for. George was so compassionate it hurt sometimes, and this was one of those times.

"Listen, they were going to kill the poor things if no one took them home today. We can put out a sign for free chickens once they are a little older if you like, and otherwise we'll take care of them until then. Chicks are real easy."

"Oh? And where did you hear that?"

"Well that's what the guy said. Chicks are easy to raise."

"George we don't have a coop, we don't have chicken feed, and, oh yeah, I know nothing about raising chickens."

"We'll learn. The internet is a boundless resource!"

"You were supposed to just get milk and eggs..."

"And I did. Milk and eggs." He held up the gallon of milk triumphantly and then indicated the chickens in the basket. Then he added sheepishly, "I also got some eggs. They are in the front seat."

"Well you best start figuring out what they need right away. They can't just stay in that basket. There's not enough room for them in there. They're just jumping all over one another."

"I know. Cute right?"

"You are missing the point, George. I've got things to do. This is your mess."

"I'm on it. Don't you worry. And when we have more eggs than you can shake a stick at..."

"I'll shake that stick at you instead!"

Fran stalked off, sighing, wondering what could have possibly gotten into her partner. But she was in this for the long haul, and sometimes partners did things impulsively. She just needed to breathe.

Fran went inside, to her office and closed the door. After a second thought, she locked it too. Her desk overlooked the backyard, which was a place of tranquility, sanctuary, and calmness. Opening her laptop, she opened a seltzer from the mini-fridge beside her desk and sipped at it. She opened her file and stared at it longingly.

While she stared, movement in the yard caught her eyes - George hefting that huge basket with him to the shed. Leaving it on the ground, he went into the shed and produced a few slats of wood and the tools to put things together. Unable to stop herself, she watched him work on it and despite herself, found herself chuckling as he would put two pieces of wood at a 90 degree angle and then struggle to nail them together. George was impulsive, but he was no woodworker, and she outright laughed when one piece of wood fell just as he drove the nail through the other, leaving the nail sticking out in the air and neither piece was together.

"Concentrate. You have work to do, Frannie." She admonished herself and tried to focus back on the file. She was a writer, and she had stories to pull together and put up for her audience. Stories that would not write themselves either.

After ten minutes, she had a few ideas on the virtual page before her. George on the other hand had managed to make a rough square out of the slats of wood at about six feet to a side. Fran saw him looking at his work appraisingly, like he had done a marvelous job. She didn't think the makeshift box would hold in the chicks though. Aside from the fact that it made the walls only six inches high, it had no bottom to it, so it was likely the chicks could just wriggle their way underneath.

However, her own assessment and his were very different. No sooner did she make that decision, George carried the basket into the box and lovingly retrieved each chick, one by one and put them into the box.

"Oh George, that's not going to work," she advised from the aerial spot she had. She resisted the urge to run down there to help him. This was his mess after all. He needed to learn what this would take.

He was only on the fifth chick when the first one managed to skirt free of the box. He scooped up the ones still in the box, but them back in the basket and then chased the last chick around the yard in a fashion that made Fran laugh uncontrollably for several minutes. He didn't have much trouble keeping up with it, but it turned erratically away from him and he wasn't prepared. When he did rescue the errant chick and returned it to the basket, he looked up at Fran's window.

"You could come and help instead of laughing you know!" he yelled up, but he was smiling and having a good time with his challenge. Fran couldn't believe he heard her laughing from that far with the window closed, but she resolved to get back to her work and let the man work in peace instead.

Some hours later, when the afternoon was waning towards evening, Fran stood from her desk, stretched and then looked out the window. George had managed to put together a more sturdy contraption at least, but still had the chicks in the basket beside him while he worked. And, she noted, he was still working at it.

Leaving her office, and taking down the four cans of seltzer and the wrappers for the cheese and crackers she had snacked on, Fran dropped them off in the kitchen and went outside.

"Looks like you are managing on this quite well." She meandered up to him and tried to keep a positive tone and look while she did. She didn't want to bruise his ego any further, even if the whole day was lost to the chicks.

"It is coming along. Just putting up the final touches."

The box, as it was now, had walls that were almost two feet high, a floor, and George had covered the floor in wood chips. He had just filled a low bucket with water and put a container in there with some chicken feed. The bag of feed just barely filled up the container George had put out.

"Want to help me get them in there?" he asked.

"I would love to George. Is this where they are going to stay?" Fran asked.

"Well... yes?"

"It was fine for today, the sun didn't get too hot, but there's no shade in there if the sun is out. That's all I'm thinking. Might be better near the tree?" Fran indicated the lone birch tree in their backyard. It was the place they went when they wanted a little picnic outside, or just a moment to themselves. One of George's most endearing qualities was looking for the quiet simple things in their lives to enjoy, and so he would have picnics and sleep on the ground outside during a lazy day.

George looked over at the tree, thinking over her suggestion, then nodded.

"I think you are right. Good idea. Can you help me?"

"I can."

Fran was a little surprised at how heavy the box was, but between the two of them, they managed to drag it over under the tree. Then George retrieved the basket from where he had left it.

"Now, they are a little skittish when you handle them, but just grab them like this," he made one hand into a shape like a cage and scooped a chick up with it, cradling it in his fingertips and brought his other hand underneath to support the chick's feet. "Easy enough, right?"

Fran smiled, nodded, and the two of them went to work. Fran was on her fourth, when she spoke up.

"Is this going to be enough for these little ones? Like is it going to be warm enough at night? How much feed will they need?" Fran realized as she helped maneuver the chicks in that she had more and more questions about them. And not for nothing, they were very cute. "How long is that bag going to last us?" she asked, indicating the nearly empty bag of feed.

She placed one down, and it would scuttle away into a corner with the others who were already there. In fact, after they had a few dozen in the box, Fran stopped to watch them interact with each other, and despite having so much room in the box, they all scurried together into the same area.

"We'll need a few more things in order to properly take care of them. I'll probably need a couple of heat lamps during the first few weeks here, but tonight should be okay. Oh and I need some netting over the top of this so that no predators get in."

"We have some boards in the basement that we could use for the night anyway, and maybe a little netting or something down there. I'll go take a look."

Fran brushed off her knees as she stood and went to investigate the basement. She found the two boards she was thinking of right away, but finding the netting took a little more of moving things around and by the time she was done, she was covered in dust and cobwebs. She lugged them out and saw that George was busily working at keeping the chicks entertained. By the time she got up to him, she realized he was full on laughing.

"This is better than TV!" he exclaimed, looking at the chicks running back and forth over one thing or another. Some had taken up sitting in the shallow water dish, while others worked on eating while still others walked over them. There was plenty of space in the box for them to not crawl over one another, but that was apparently what they did. Fran set down the wood and the netting and just enjoyed watching the show herself for a bit.

"Well, I found this all. Should be enough for tonight anyway." True enough, it was already starting to get dark. "Here, help with the net."

Between the two of them it was easy enough to get the net on, and while it didn't cover the entire box, it covered enough that they could use the two boards to cover the rest. They didn't really want to leave too much open space for predators to have a good view in there anyway.

"Are they going to be all right out here, do you think?" George asked as they started to head to the house.

"Now's the wrong time to be asking that George. The right time would've been before you brought them home. Remember?"

"Right. Okay fine. See you all in the morning. I'll be back. I promise."

Fran found herself wondering about the small army of chicks herself, but tried to put it out of her mind while they put together a simple dinner - a couple of frozen meals out of the freezer. It wasn't exactly the best meal, but where they had been busy all day, she decided working further in the kitchen on dinner wasn't worth the effort.

George elected to sleep on the couch with the window open so that he could hear for any trouble outside. Fran knew better than to argue with him, even though she felt it was quite unnecessary. Fran had a little trouble sleeping without George in bed with her, but eventually she drifted off.

Fran woke to a noise that wasn't normal to her. It wasn't especially loud, just persistent and in her half-awake state, she wasn't sure it was a real sound. She shook off the residue of her rest, and sat and listened.

Scratch, scratch, scratch.

There it was. She was sure she heard it, but it still didn't make any sense to her. She stood and walked to the wall. Was the sound coming from there? She put her hand to the wall to feel as well.

Scratch. Scratch. Scratch.

She drew her hand back in surprise. What could it possibly be?

"George!" Fran called out, hoping he was already awake. It was now that she noticed it was much later than her normal waking time. The clock read ten in the morning. Why hadn't he woken her up?

There was no response to her call, and the scratching happened again. Could one of the chicks gotten in the house? Or worse, gotten into the wall? But how?

"George!" she called again, this time heading out of the room and down the stairs. She stopped about two steps from the ground floor. "George!" she cried out, now panicking.

All of the chickens were in the house!

George still didn't respond to her cries, and when she looked out the front door, she saw that the van was gone. Carefully she navigated her way through the throng of yellow puff balls on the ground, nearly falling several times to avoid stepping on them, but they seemed oblivious to her plight.

"How did you all get in here?" she asked, still dodging through them, step by step. She needed coffee. Tea. Whiskey maybe.

Finally getting to the kitchen, she found it was similarly overrun with the chicks, and tried her best to just keep going through what she needed to get her coffee. The chicks were on the floor, on the kitchen chairs and table. On the counter. Everywhere. And they were, for the most part, completely unaware of the frustration they were causing her.

Getting the coffee going was an exercise in small madness, shuffling through to the coffee maker, grabbing the pot and shuffling to the sink, scooping out the two trapped chicks in the sink, filling the pot, emptying the pot into the reservoir, then grabbing the coffee and the filters and finally scooping some in and starting the coffee maker. While it brewed, she decided to investigate what happened outdoors.

As she emerged from the house though, she saw the van coming up their long driveway. A glance over at the box they had painstakingly made the day before, she saw both pieces of wood shoved off the sides and the netting seemed to be completely gone. The van came to a stop and George erupted from it with apologies flowing.

"I know. I'm sorry. That's no way for you to start your day. It... it was supposed to be so much easier, but the chicks... They were so cold last night. You should have seen them..."

"I do see them. They are everywhere, George. Everywhere. Wait. Where did you go?"

George had on his sheepish look again as she asked, and his eyes flicked to the house. "Umm... I've got to get these chickens fed," he said, dodged around her, around her question. He was at the door when he stopped, ran back to the van and grabbed a bag of chicken feed from the back.

"I ran out of food. They really are voracious eaters..."

"We only had them for the night. Shouldn't they have been sleeping."

"Well, as I said, they were so cold out there. I had to bring them in, and then it was a whole new place for them to explore and... well one thing led to another and now they are everywhere."

"Yes. Everywhere. Like in the walls. How are we going to get them out?"

"I don't know yet. I didn't expect this to happen you know."

"I'm well aware of that, yes," she said, holding the door open for him because he was standing there with a bag of chicken feed that was too heavy for him to be lugging around. He nodded his thanks, went inside and started dumping the feed on the ground.

"What are you doing?" she cried out, too late to stop him.

"They're hungry!"

"But you don't need to spill it over the floor like that."

"It will take too long to get them back in the box though. They'll be wasting away to nothing by then."

Fran couldn't ignore the fact that the chicks came running at him while he dumped a little feed at a time over the floor. This was her chance to scoop them up one by one and bring them back outside.

"The chickens need to stay out in the box, George. This is ridiculous!"

"Fine. But they aren't going to like that."

"They're chickens!" She started crying, picking up two chickens and carrying them outside. As she placed them in the box, she nearly collapsed on the ground. What were these chickens doing to them? She didn't understand.

The basket he brought them home in was right next to her. She scooped it up and returned to get as many of the chickens as she could in the basket. That seemed better than taking hundreds of trips back and forth. However, by the time she got back, there was no sign of the chickens in the front of the house. She could hear George in the kitchen there and followed after him.

He was sitting in a chair at the table, the bag of feed already half empty. There were chicks climbing all over one another, up his legs, and onto his lap. He had handfuls of the feed that he was handing out, trying to get as many different chickens as he could. To Fran's amazement, he didn't look at all frazzled or discouraged, he just fed a few, grabbed a new handful and fed a few more, and so on.

Fran scooped as many as she could into the basket, trying to get the ones he had already fed and stowed them away quickly. Luckily it appeared that most of the errant birds were in the kitchen by now, drawn together by that innate need for food, so it was easy enough to collect them.

"How are you ever going to keep track of all these?" she asked once the last one was collected. They walked together out to the box and set them all free in there.

"I don't know. They might be more than I bargained for, but they are a lot of fun."

"This is not what I would call fun. Oh, and you have some cleaning up to do inside. Those birds made quite the mess."

"I know. I will."

They left the issue alone and she helped him set up the heat lamps he bought at the store and brought out the six other bags of feed he had picked up too. She was glad he had thought that much ahead, but it still seemed like it wouldn't be enough.

That night, after he had cleaned up completely from their mess, after she had caved in and helped out, they went to bed. Fran was just about asleep, but then she heard it again.

Scratch, scratch, scratch. From behind the wall.

Ocean Adventure

When Liz's parents said they were going on an adventure, she didn't realize that they meant to stick her on some rickety boat and send her off by herself. Alone. Liz thought the idea was preposterous, ridiculous, and many other four-syllable words that conveyed exactly what she thought.

Liz hated to go outside. She liked looking at nature well enough - from behind the safety of her bedroom window - but being outside? That was just no good at all. Worse yet, her parents gave her all of two days notice for the trip, and also let her know she'd be on her own. Given the eyes her parents shared for each other, she assumed she wanted to know nothing about their plans. So she didn't ask, and they only shared bits and pieces that made her shudder. Just as well to be on a boat, so she could drown herself at the thought of her parents like that. Yuck.

Liz had never been on a boat of any size before - not a canoe, raft, sailboat or yacht. Nothing. She was quite content to read about the adventures that can come from them, but she had no intentions of meeting any giants on random islands, nor strange creatures from lands long forgotten in any place but her books. And she read plenty, that was for sure. She loved to curl up in the chair at her desk and read, or curl up in her bed and read. Or be anywhere inside, safe, and read. Reading was her passion. Going on a boat, much less so. Wasn't even on her list, to be sure.

The day came for her to leave, and she tugged along a bookbag that she could barely manage on her own. Her father helped her with the bag, grunted once and stared at her.

"Packing rocks now?"

"They're books, Dad," she said, lengthening his name into three syllables.

"You know there's a whole world out there? There's going to be others on the boat your age?"

"Yeah, I know." She didn't add that she wasn't interested in connecting with any of *those* people. That sounded like a different form of torture. Again - better to jump ship - she thought melodramatically.

"Well, you're going to have fun. You'll see. It will be a lot easier if you assume you will too. Half the fun of an adventure is not knowing everything."

"Sure. The other half is just surviving."

Her dad laughed, nodding. "Right. If you survive, you'll have had a rocking good time I bet!"

She glared at him again. She was joking. And he was joking, right? She was suddenly not so sure and panic was setting in. "Do I have to go?"

He smiled, touched her shoulder gently and nodded. "Yes. Yes, you do. You've spent too much time up in that room of yours getting lost in your books. It is time for you to experience some of those stories for yourself."

"Well, if I don't come back, just know that I told you I didn't want to go. So it would be your fault."

"And if you do come back and had a good time, that would also be my fault. I'll take my chances."

OFF THEY DROVE TO THE wharf. To the docks. To the gateway to hell for all she knew. A large sign proclaiming the Seaport passed over the car as they entered, and while there were things to look at - buildings with various nautical-themed murals, and sculptures and relics of the vast unknown of the ocean - anchors and fish, sharks, and whales - Liz just wanted to close her eyes and make them all go away.

Eventually, they parked the car in a mostly-empty parking lot with an assortment of pickup trucks that looked like they smelled like fish and Liz got out of the car and all she could smell was ocean and seaweed and fish. She looked at her parents who were not getting out of the car.

"So you're just leaving me here in the parking lot?" She was not impressed.

Her father indicated a building off next to the parking lot with a large sign in front of it, reading "Nautical Adventures" with an arrow pointing to the building. Liz grabbed her bag, dragged it melodramatically from the car, let it hit the ground hard before picking it up again. While she didn't love damaging her books, she also wanted to punish her parents for treating her like this.

Liz grumbled, grudgingly walked away from the car and went into the building-that-smelled-more-like-fish-than-the-parking-lot and said good bye to her parents forever for as far as she was concerned. Once inside, it took her eyes a moment to adjust to the difference in light. Straight ahead, there was a desk with a woman in a t-shirt that advertised "Nautical Adventures" on it.

"READY FOR YOUR ADVENTURE?" she called out, way too excited for a random weekend day, for too early in the morning. For a teenager at any time. Liz grumbled something under her breath, brought up the best smile she could muster.

"Yeah. I guess. My parents signed me up."

"Enthusiastic! That's great. We love to have newcomers. Ever been sailing?"

"Never."

"Oh good. You're going to love it. And I mean that. You will love it."

"I doubt that."

"You can doubt it. I'll believe it for the two of us. Name?"

"Liz."

"Liz. Got it. Yup, you are right here in the category of newcomers. To be honest, you're the only one on today's trip. Newcomer that is. We've got a full boat otherwise. Six other teens - but they are all old hands at this. Just like you'll be I bet. Is that your bag?"

Liz resisted retorting with a snappy comment, and just nodded.

"Good. I hope it isn't heavy or it might break through the floorboards."

Liz couldn't stop the flash of panic from showing on her eyes. The woman smiled reassuringly.

"I'm joking. Our boat is state of the art, and none of the floorboards are rotting, I assure you."

Liz was sure she didn't want to get on any boat, rotting floorboards or not. But her parents had already left the parking lot. And she was the only teenager in the world without a cell phone. So she was on her own. Forever.

"Ok. You are all signed in."

Liz wondered what that process actually was, because the woman had only been talking to her, there was no computer or anything in front of her - just a piece of paper with a few names on it. "Come on back with me. Name is Angie by the way."

"Pleased to meet you, Angie," Liz said by reflex.

Angie led the way through the building, down a narrow hall with four closed doors and frosted glass with names of people on them she didn't recognize. At the end of the hall was another door that led back outside, though instead of the parking lot, she was in a lot for boats. And really it was just one boat. A sailboat.

THE BOAT GLEAMED FRESHLY white and blue, as if they had just painted it. The sails were all wrapped up, and a heavyset man bustled about on the boat with purpose. He moved things around, set up cushions, tied or untied ropes, seemingly at random. Liz didn't know what to make of any of it.

Angie waved and the man looked up with a broad smile, whipped a captain's cap out from his pocket and thrust it on his head. He waved back as he stepped out from behind the wheel. "Ahoy Angie," he called out.

"Ahoy Bert."

Bert? Captain Bert. That was not what she expected.

"Got a first timer here Bert. Take good care of her. She thinks the world ends at the horizon."

"No I do not!" Liz protested, walking into the setup.

"Well, we'll teach her right on that one. No worries. Come on aboard landlubber!" Bert gave Liz an impossibly wide smile that for all of its strangeness looked genuine. She wasn't going to be comfortable with being on a boat, for sure, but at least his smile was reassuring. Liz swung her bag over the wall of the boat and it crashed against the side. Liz winced. Bert smiled.

"Bit heavy for ya?"

"Yeah," she said, ducking her head down and stepping into the boat awkwardly.

"Here, let me help ya." He took it as if it was no heavier than a pillow, and led her into the deck below. "You can stow this down here," he said, putting the bag on a single cot in the wall. Above it was a second cot, and on the other side of the tiny hallway, were two more cots. Each had a thin privacy curtain that she supposed was to give people the illusion they were in coffins. Dead. Something like that.

Bert caught her looking at the bed in dread.

"Oh don't worry. We aren't going to be out that long anyway. Only if we get blown off course would you need one of these." Bert smiled.

Liz grimaced at the thought. She wondered if she would have a light to read by, and was surprised that each bed did have a small light in there. The boat might not have much, but light to read by was a luxury she wasn't prepared to live without.

"Come on up and I'll give you the grand tour. This here's the sleeping quarters. There's eight beds on this here boat. Four here, four over there." He indicated the opposite end of the boat. "The galley - the kitchen - is down at that end. We'll likely eat up top, since the weather is supposed to be great today. The head is over here," he indicated back behind them, then led the way back out.

Climbing back up to the top, he showed her around, using terms she didn't know and certainly wouldn't remember. He showed her where the life jackets were. She was surprised he didn't require her to put one on, and was too nervous to ask for one for herself.

"Here's a spot you can sit when we set off. When moving about, make sure you have a hand on this railing here." He indicated a railing that ran along the whole of the boat on the inside of the boat, away from the side. The railing on the side of the boat was just a small rope. Liz thought that the rope would be very useless in protecting her from falling off the boat into the water.

THE WIND WHIPPED BY the boat as Liz sat down, sitting on a flotation cushion out of the way of the bustling activity. Then, Liz saw a small crowd of teenagers coming down the dock. All girls, she saw with some relief. That relief went away when she caught a sneer from the first one to make eye contact with her. She said something to the others and they all laughed. Liz didn't know what she had done wrong already, but she wanted to crawl up and head below decks with her books.

They came on the boat one at a time, formally asking Bert for permission to "Come aboard" which he gave to them all individually, saluting them as they came on. They sat down without prompting at various cushions around the boat. Only one of the girls was next to her, but it was the one who had made eye contact with her. The one who sneered.

Liz reluctantly extended her hand.

"Liz," she said.

"Marta," the girl responded, looking down at her feet and around on the boat at every place except toward Liz. She did not take Liz's hand and did not make further eye contact with her. Liz thought it was very rude of her to behave that way.

And just like that, Liz would have felt much better either in the water away from Marta, or with Marta in the water away from her. Since she wasn't fond of swimming, she thought Marta would be better off in the water. Definitely.

"Alright folks, hold on to your railings and we'll set off straight away."

Captain Bert started the engine and directed the boat away from the docks, and then out from the harbor where it rested. Soon enough, Liz found herself gazing out at ocean all around except for the land where they just left. Panic had never left her, she realized, just hid in her gut and was now ready to burst from her. She closed her eyes, clenched the railing as tightly as she could, wishing for the sensation to go away.

"Tensing up isn't going to help." Marta said, almost confidingly, next to her. "Relax. The nausea will pass."

Liz opened her eyes for a second and saw that Marta was giving her some sympathetic eyes. "What would you care?" Liz managed.

"If you throw up, there's a good chance it'll get on me."

Liz managed to laugh a little, Marta did as well.

It was a small laugh, but it at least set Liz a little more at ease. Marta patted her hand, and Liz tried to clench a little less hard. The turmoil in her gut wasn't fading, at least not yet.

Suddenly the engine stopped completely. Panic rose in Liz again and she looked back at Bert, expecting to see clouds of black smoke pouring out from the back of the boat. What she saw instead was Bert leaving the wheel entirely and getting up to unfurl the sails.

"Alright, what happens now?" he asked expectantly of everyone around.

"Now we go!" the other teens gasped, smiling, excitement on their faces.

"Right. Remember, keep your head down when the mast swings or it'll give you a good walloping. No one wants a walloping right?"

"Right!" they chorused again. Liz looked back and was surprised to see the smile on Marta's face.

The flutter of nervousness in Liz's gut wasn't abating, and as she realized they would be soon under sail power, she wondered how much worse this was going to get. She wanted to ask Marta, so that she would know what to expect. Or to stay silent and just experience it, like her father had suggested. She kept her lips shut though, anticipating the worst and also not wanting to lose what she had for breakfast.

THE BOAT DIDN'T DO much until Bert got back to the wheel. Then, as he brought the mast around, all of a sudden it snapped as if it was putting up a military salute. Liz felt like they were getting blown by a hurricane. The boat raced off at a hundred miles an hour, and she couldn't breathe. The little strip of land in the distance faded away entirely, and all she could feel were the waves beneath the boat, the wind blowing, the air, the spray from the sea, and all of the world around her. She wanted it to be horrible.

But it wasn't.

The first couple of jostles by the waves were jarring, painful, like they were running into a brick wall over and over. But once they were underway, Liz felt the rhythm of it, and while the panic inside her was still there, there was something else overriding it all. She couldn't put a finger on it, couldn't really understand it. It was spreading through her like the ocean spreading out across the horizon. And then?

Liz found herself smiling. And when the other girls screamed as they hit a wave, she screamed with them. Every jolt and jump the boat made was another beam of excitement. The spray of the ocean, at first was annoying and she would wipe it away urgently, only to quickly bring her hand back to the safety line. Then it became a part of her. The saltiness filled her senses, and she blinked with wonder and joy each time the spray hit her face. It felt for all the world a joy unto itself.

AFTER A LONG TIME, Bert let the sail drop and the boat just set calmly in the water, resting just as if it hadn't been running through the water like some water horse with a purpose. Bert went below deck.

Marta looked back at Liz. "Feeling better?"

Liz nodded. Somewhere along the way, her nausea had passed. So had her pessimisms, dreads, and horrors. All that was left was the enjoyment. The fun. She was amazed.

"How long are we out here?"

"For as long as you want," Marta said, holding Liz's hand.

That sounded like a lot of fun. Bert came back, and passed out sandwiches and drinks, chips and fruit to all of the passengers. Liz, who would have ordinarily scoffed at such a lunch, took each piece and ate along with the others. And while they ate, the sun sparkled on the water, the waves lapped at the boat, and a strange looking fish came swimming by. Liz had never seen anything like it before. It looked like a weird surfboard without anyone to ride on it.

"Sunfish," Bert said from behind her, as he tugged at a line, adjusting one thing or another that she knew nothing about. She nodded, still chewing away at her lunch.

Once everyone was done, Bert set up the sail again and once again the boat was racing through the ocean, beating back waves, launching through the air, galloping like the horse it was. Liz could barely hold her breath, cried out laughing all the way. The others around her laughed and played, ducking under the mast and watching out for any fish or dolphins as they went. Liz saw nothing but the waves though, and couldn't imagine a greater joy in her.

They came back to the docks as the sun was coming down to set. The sky was painted in such a wide array of colors, the seagulls called overhead, the wind played with Liz's hair. Stunned as she was, she barely noticed as Bert tied the boat to the dock and the others started to disembark. Liz finally stood, unsteady on her feet, and walked off herself. She was halfway down the dock when Bert called her back.

"You forgot your bag, Liz."

She didn't want to admit the adventure was done. Still, Liz turned back and took the bag from him. Filled with books, adventures in the mind. And she wondered if any of them would be the same ever again.

Somewhere along the way, Liz found a love for the ocean. And her parents were going to have to live with that. For the rest of their lives.

Hope

Hope.

It was the one word I came back to every time I faced situations like this. Hope was the only thing that could possibly see us through to success, or to survive, to live another day. Hope was what drove us forward.

The situation today, though, was dire. And I wasn't sure hope would be enough.

I'm the lone guardian of the water watchtower - a tower of light built to guide ships home through turbulent and clear weather both. The tower is built on a rocky island some kilometers off shore and had a light that reflected off of the mirrors around it and pierced through even the densest fog, the most sheeting rain, and the most blanketing snow. And here in the north, we got them all. Sometimes in the span of one day we got them all.

The tower stood some forty feet above the island, and while the island laid low in the ocean, it remained stalwart for hundreds of years. I was the fifth such guardian to inhabit the watchtower, and I expected it would stand easily for five more, other than the need for hope. Because each time we need hope, I felt the tower's resoluteness waiver. And maybe, just maybe it would falter one of these days. I hoped it wasn't while I was here, or even any of my descendants. But such is hope. It can only do so much.

The storm coming at me was a violent one. I'd seen the storm clouds in the distance for weeks. It was slow moving, destructive, and ready for vengeance against the tower. Birds fled from it. Whales and fish swum away. Now, between the tower and the storm, there was only open ocean. And it seemed determined to throw the whole of the ocean at me in addition to the precipitation. All I could do was let it come though.

The waves crested five meters easily, well above the shoreline, well above the door to the tower. I expected the bottom floor to be completely flooded. I expected my boat that I used to go to the mainland would be rent to pieces. I expected the small dock where the boat was tied up would be torn from the island and sent plummeting to the depths before long as well. The rocks however, those would stay. No matter how powerful the storm, the rocks always stayed. They were moored to the island with some ancient strength of dirt and stone that simply could not dislodge them. Or, at least had never been dislodged before.

LIGHTNING STREAKED the sky, wind whipped the air around, rain started falling and snow, and ice. The temperature was right at that perfect spot where you could get anything, and the storm would show you just how strong and masterful it was by giving it all to you. However, despite the horrible weather, this was just the edge. I still could see hope in the form of clear skies behind me. I could see some glimmer of hope in the sky, a sun that wouldn't perish. Maybe the storm would blow past and I would be looking at the sun again soon. Maybe not. That remained to be seen.

Waves crashed against the rocks on the island, threatened to break the rocks in two, but the rocks refused to break, and told the waves to break instead. And they did. One after another, broken upon the shore, and while water leaped on to the shore, it would recede in time. This was why I wasn't too concerned about flooding on the ground floor. It had flooded before; it would flood again in the future. I didn't store anything down there beyond immediate needs, so if it flooded, nothing would be lost. The loss of my boat was a bigger concern that I didn't have an immediate fix for.

Lightning streaked across the sky again, arcing from one spot to the next, and not coming down to the ocean so far as I could tell. Was it scared of the ocean? I wondered. The storm was still just the edge for me; it was so slow moving I wouldn't be surprised if I could run across clear land faster than it. Still, better to be inside a stalwart tower. I hoped. I wondered if maybe I should have taken the boat to shore before the seas got so rough. It was too late for that by days now. The seas had turned inhospitable over a week ago. Had it really been that long? Stormy seas on clear days were dangerous to all in the ocean. I probably would have foundered in that tiny boat had I even tried to get back. No, it was safer to stay. Safer for me. Safer for any captain who tried to find their way through this god-forsaken storm. I doubted anyone would be at sea that could be saved, but if I could give them a glimmer of hope, well, that would be something. And if they survived to the mainland, well, that would be worth all of the hope in the world.

Storms like this caused me all kinds of worry that there was foul play at hand. How could a storm be this severe and so slow moving if not by the hand of some sinister force? But then, what sinister force could command the weather at all? None that I had ever seen first hand. The possibility was out there though. The possibility that something else was at work here that I just didn't understand. That I couldn't comprehend.

ANOTHER ARC OF LIGHTNING. And another. Followed very quickly with such thunderous booms that I had never heard before. The storm was very nearly upon me. All of the windows were boarded up, all of the loose things secured. Even the light at the top of the tower was sheltered behind its protective shell. It could withstand a lot - but it was not impenetrable. Even though nothing had ever damaged or destroyed it before, I had visions of it being destroyed that littered my dreams. I also had seen the destruction of the tower in my dreams. I hoped they would not come true.

The storm clouds came over the tower like a swarm of insects that blotted out the sky in slow motion. The clouds roiled and burned, flashed and resonated around me. They were low as well, which made them all the more looming. All the more terrible. In the flashes of lightning, I could see movement in the clouds, though whether there were things in the sky or if it was just a trick of the light, I could not say for sure. Still, the storm felt all the world of evil, and I hoped I could just see my way to the other side of it. But the only way to the other side was through, and the only way through was to stay put and let it wash over the tower, over the island, and over the ocean that threatened to destroy anything in its path.

The waves were cresting six, maybe seven meters now, fully up over the bottom floor of the tower and each time they struck the land, it made the whole tower shake and shiver. I put my hands on the stone of the tower, to lend it what moral support I could. Not that it would actually help or matter in the end, but the things that protect us, deserve our support in turn. It was the only thing I could actually do, nothing could stop this apocalypse. I could only watch as it came.

More flashes in the sky, more phantasms flying by. Witches? That seemed too far-fetched, but that was the image in my head. Stories from my childhood of people hunting and eating other people, weaving magic in unnatural ways. Stories all. And inaccurate to the extreme. I knew plenty of witches, and none of them once tried to eat another person. Also, their magic was largely not so potent, certainly not so potent as the storm. Still, that was the image in my head. Sinister beings hidden among the clouds, flying through it. How anything could fly in such terribly powerful winds and rain, through the lightning, defied any realm of logic I could find in my soul. No, they were just phantasms. Just imaginations, trying to make a real storm into some fantastic, otherworldly creation.

ANOTHER FLASH OF LIGHTNING, a crash of thunder, the buffeting of winds, the punches of waves shook my whole world. Was that a crack? I thought I heard something beyond all of it, but it was impossible to hear anything but the storm. Still, I thought I heard it, and so I moved from my spot, inspecting every inch of the tower that I could safely do. As I moved from the top floor sanctuary though, I could feel the difference. The boards on the second floor were torn away, the windows broken, and now wind and rain and snow whipped into the second floor, and waves plummeted in as if they came from the sky itself. The second floor was lost. It was where most of my provisions were - not all - but most. I would have only a few days to live out the storm, and if it didn't take me, well, then maybe lack of food, lack of water would. It would be a horrible way for it all to end, after all this time. Why didn't I go to shore?

I returned to the sanctuary, closed and boarded the door shut. I returned to my chair, an ancient thing that had been here since the first days of the tower's opening. It was well used, but sturdy, comfortable - having had the stuffing replaced every few years was a luxury I could justify well since I spent so much time in it. It gave me a view all around from the tower top, and allowed me to control the tower's light with very little effort. This was a huge boon, for there were plenty of times when effort from storms around the tower made everything more difficult.

I remembered a storm from my youth where there were a dozen ships in my view stuck and floundering out there, and a thirteenth out there trying their best to rescue those they could. It was a lost cause, and I could see all of it unfold from the top of the tower, unable to affect the outcome at all. Still, it was a difficult day, and controlling the light was of the most importance. Had I not been there to direct the people trying to save the others, surely they would have all been lost. Unfortunately, even with my help, so many still perished that day. That was a fast storm. Terrible in power, and ruthless in strength, and it tore apart eight of the ships in no time, and sank two others. Forty people were saved; hundreds lost. But for my work, all of them would have died, including the twenty on the boat out there trying to save the others.

A crash against the tower directly shook me out of my reminiscing. The tower could take the waves. Was constructed to let the waves splash over her like any of the rocks below. Break up the wave, send it crying back into the ocean. But these waves were strong. I could feel it as each pounding wave struck. As each time they struck, I could foresee the destruction of the tower take place in my mind's eye.

THE PRECIPITATION EDDIED, and the wind even lessened some. The waves receded. But above me, in the clouds, the storm still raged. It was holding its strength. Building up to hit the island with a force stronger yet, I figured. Some would call it the eye of the storm. It was far from calm. Certainly didn't feel any better, because it was a constant threat of what was yet to come. What was left to befall the tower, the island, the rocks, and me.

I rested in that span when the storm was resting. If it would build up its strength, then so would I. The thunder and lightning was still close, but not right on top of me. Was at least distant enough that the stone of the tower muffled them a little.

I came to some time later. I wasn't sure if it was day or night. It had been dark for so long already and I could see no sign of lightness anywhere, in any direction. This was the part of the storm that took all hope from everything and left only despair. The storm had started up again in force, crashing, and thrashing, rending everything in sight.

For all of the endurance of the tower, and of the island it rested on, I wondered how the storm would destroy all of the mainland with its force. The buildings others lived in were not so stalwart, and the other structures were rarely so strong that they could withstand forces like this, and certainly not for long. The only thing they had going was the storm would likely lose strength over the land. The coastal communities were probably in for a rough night ahead - if it was night. I still didn't have a good sense of time. Time didn't really matter.

More crashing waves hit the tower, shaking it to the bones, to my bones. Again, I put my hand on the wall, willing it to take the hits, but to stay put. Never have I felt so powerless as this. But when it is all you have left, then it is what you do, both to make the time pass, and to feel like you are more than an ant in this vast world.

Hope was gone by then. Despair was overtaking everything. I barely had a second's reprieve between thunder and the flashes of lightning were so constant, it might have been coming from all around me. Indeed, I could see nearly all the way to the horizon for how constant the brightness from the lightning was. Still, it was an illusion like the witches. I could see no further than my arm had I been out there in it. And to this point, I was inside. And as safe as I could be, I hoped.

More crashing. More shaking. Another crack? Was it? What was left to break except for the tower itself I wondered. I could not afford to investigate though, leaving my sanctuary would expose me to whatever was happening on the second floor, and it was already lost. And since it was already lost, I might as well stay put. Might as well keep myself as safe as possible.

The wind buffeted the tower anew, shaking it in ways that the waves could not and for a brief moment, I thought the whole top of the tower would fly off, disconnected and take me away. Into the ocean no doubt, but away nonetheless. Still, it didn't, and it was just another fancy of my mind as it tried to understand the chaos of the storm.

OFF IN THE DISTANCE, nearly at the edge of the horizon that I could see, I swore I could see a bit of a lighter colored cloud. It was too far off to be sure, but it was the last glimmer of hope for me. The last potential of getting through this, surviving. I poured myself a glass of water. It was the first I had had since the start of the storm. It was a superstition of mine to not drink until I saw the storm's farthest edge, and I had finally reached that point. It was still far off, but at least I could see it coming.

On and on the storm raged. Another crash and a terrible shake of the tower. I hoped it would survive these last few hours. It would be a shame to falter when salvation was just in sight. Just nearly close enough to grasp. As a concept. It was still kilometers away, for sure.

I drank down the water in one gasp. I was parched. I had been holding my breath for as long as I could each breath. Like I wouldn't get another breath if I tried, so I better hold on to it. But that was silly, the air was still there. So was the water. Waiting did nothing but make me suffer for it. But it was what I did, even if it didn't make sense.

The edge of the storm was clear now, and beyond it, I could see it was past dawn. The sun shone underneath the clouds as it started to rise in the east. It was glorious to perceive and gave a weird light to the storm, where it was impossibly dark due to the clouds, but the rain and snow, and the wind I dare say, were lit up by the sun and made everything shimmer and shine. Even the coating of ice blanketing the exterior shone brightly. If only for a few minutes, then the sun was above the line of the storm clouds and I was again in darkness. But the light was out there, if far away. I could wait out the rest of the storm. Hope could get me there. I was certain of it.

Another crash. How many was that? Ten? Forty? A hundred? I had lost count. I just knew it was a lot. I could hear water sloshing around. Probably on the floor below. How much would be left? Would there even be a floor for me to descend to? I didn't know.

It might have been hours before the storm finally passed, but it still felt like days. When it did pass, the storm gave one final push at the tower and I thought for sure it would collapse. Somehow, however, it did not. The sun broke through the storm clouds triumphantly. Saying "Here I am!" with such brightness, I could almost forget that it was not so powerful as to drive away the storm faster. It was well past the noon hour though, so it had been hours. I looked out at the seas, and they would be stormy for days still, but maybe passable once the storm moved on. Passable to those with a boat. And I was almost certainly without one now.

I stayed in that room for some time longer, not wanting to see the destruction of the bottom floors until I was ready to deal with it. I drank another glass of water. Ate some salted fish. Sat in my chair. Listened as the lingering wind blew through the holes and sent eerie echoes through the whole of the tower. Whatever the destruction below, the sanctuary had persevered. And within it, so did I. I could have hoped for more, but that would have been some kind of hubris. I was thankful to have survived. And the rest, well the rest could be rebuilt, and left for history to remember. Someone should remember anyway.

Pieces

Thirty years ago, after my son's birthday party, he was building his very first Lego set. It was an impressive castle, the largest of its kind and the most impressive gift he had ever been given. Sure, he was only six at the time so my wife and I, we had to help him with it because it was too large for his attention span.

I was not blessed with calm hands though, and when they shake, sometimes, I lose the grip on what I've been holding. Wouldn't you know it that while holding one of those individual pieces that I would lose my hold on it and send it flying out of sight. There was most definitely a meltdown, most definitely many apologies, and I quite earnestly considered going to the store to buy a second building set to replace the one lost piece because it was, as luck would have it, one of those special bricks that only came in that one set.

Of course, we searched the room for the lost piece, and the rooms nearby, and all over that blasted apartment because I was not going to disappoint my son like that. Eventually, unable to find it, we simply kept building it without that single piece. My son was heartbroken, so were my wife and I, and I was sure that this was one of those moments that would form into a core memory for him. This would define who he was as a child, who we were as parents in his eyes.

Mike, our son, lost interest in the building of the set some few minutes later, even though we enthusiastically continued with him on it until he was ready for bed. Sharon put him to bed, and I sat there in front of the project like it was a riddle to be solved. Could we even build the rest of it without that missing piece? Wasn't that some kind of sacrilege? Wasn't that inviting a kind of chaos into our lives that could not result in anything positive or good?

When Sharon came out of the bedroom later, she found me eagerly building at it because I just couldn't stop myself.

"You know that's his toy right?"

"Yeah... He's not going to enjoy it until it is built though. These are really for the adults to put together and the children to play with afterward."

Sharon knew better than to argue with me and sent herself off to bed to read a book or something. I was determined to just do "a little more" a few times, and then it was past midnight and the entire project was done save for that one stupid missing piece. That piece was so obviously key to the whole castle. Had a catapult sent a rock through a key piece of the wall, that was precisely where it would've needed to hit.

Exhausted and knowing that Mike would be up in a few short hours, I did send myself to bed. Sharon was asleep with her reading light on, so I put away her book, shut off the light and climbed into bed shortly afterward.

This is because the next day after building it, Mike was so upset that I built the whole thing without him, that he destroyed that set. He sent pieces flying everywhere in his rage. It was all I could do to prevent him from setting fire to our apartment to cleanse it, that was how far along in his grief he was. As a result, I thought it was best that I store the set away forever, and never let him see it again.

Sharon and I divorced when he was just out of high school. I can't say it had anything to do with the Lego set piece, but I'm not ruling it out. I can't imagine what the judge would have said to a complaint like "Lost a piece to our son's first Lego set," but it was probably like "Send him to jail for the rest of his life." It would have been fitting I suppose. But really it was just that she and I had found we didn't have much in common after we were done with the business of raising him, and while I wouldn't exactly call it an amicable break, at least she still calls to make sure I'm not dying in a gutter from time to time.

Mike calls too, ostensibly to tell me about his latest girlfriend, some success at work, some blunder a neighbor walked into, or some other nonsense. I know he's really just checking on his old man. It's sweet. Really it is.

Oh I was talking about the divorce. It was important because that's when I pulled out the Lego set that had been destroyed so many years previous. I figured when he had flailed all over it that there would be more pieces that had gone missing, but the internet had proven to be a very useful resource in its time and I learned all about being able to get lost instructions booklets and missing pieces - even rare ones.

Armed with all of these tools at hand, I built up that set and made careful note as I went as to which pieces were missing. I was only on the tenth instruction when I found the step with the ill-fated piece that had gone missing. I knew which piece it was of course, and checked the piles I had to make sure it hadn't reemerged over the years, but it wasn't there. So I made the note to look for it later, and then continued building. As I said, I expected there were other missing pieces, because once one piece is missing, is it really that important to find them all?

As luck would have it though, I did have every single other piece. Not a single one missing. Not a single one, other than the one I had dropped.

The internet however, should have been the savior of the project, so I sent in the details of what I was looking for and some vendor out of Ireland claimed to have it for the low low price of seventeen dollars, plus shipping. Seventeen dollars for a single Lego piece that would probably have no meaning to anyone but me at that point. Somehow, I managed to avoid the shame of ordering it and kept looking around. I didn't find anyone else with it that day, but I did find one the next for ten, and while that still seemed outrageous, I couldn't argue that it was a rare piece. I put in the order.

Some days later, the package arrived in a bubble mailer and I excitedly tore it open, only to find out that it wasn't actually the right piece. It was the piece's opposite, for another facade of the same castle and while it was visually similar, there was no doubt that it was the reflection of what I needed. This was my first lesson about buying Legos off of the internet. I would like to say it was the only one I needed. That would be a lie however.

Did you know that my first purchase of the missing Lego was twelve years ago? And change. Maybe a little more than twelve actually. I have managed to buy the wrong piece countless times over the years, including one amazing mistake where I bought the exact same set, supposedly never opened, just so I could have that one piece. Imagine my dismay when I learned the set had been opened and also didn't have the piece in question.

Oh sure, there were buyer protections for most of these and I was able to send the bulk of them back for most of my money in return. I would love to say I got all of my money back, but that would have been a lie. No, I lost a fair bit of money on this project. A project to find the missing piece and then restore the family I had lost all those years ago. But it didn't seem like it was meant to be.

So let's stop reminiscing and get to the heart of the issue. Today, my son came by with his partner and their son. My grandson. He was the spitting image of Mike when he was born of course, how could he not be? And now at less than a year, they were still doting over him as new parents did. I got a chance to hold the little tyke, play peek-a-boo and all manner of other things that infants will usually laugh at. I was in the middle of one of those games when Mike opened the door to his old room.

"Wait," I said, too late to stop him and he looked inside before he turned around. And when he did turn around, I saw he was crying.

"What... what is it Mike?"

"The Lego set? You kept it all these years?"

I nodded. "Of course I did."

His partner came to hold him, unsure of where this sudden burst of crying came from.

"I was so angry..." he said, sobbing. "I didn't understand anything back then about me. About what was going on."

"Neither did I. I was a pretty bad father I guess for losing that piece on you. If I hadn't, maybe you wouldn't have broken it up the next morning."

"That's not it. I was angry that you built it without me."

"What?"

"I wanted to build it with you, Dad." Mike was getting closer to holding his sobs in check. "It took me a long time to understand that. It was never about playing with the finished set. It was about building it with you."

I looked down at my lap.

"But you were tired, couldn't concentrate on the project anymore. Your mother put you to bed."

"Yes. And that's when you should've stopped working on it."

I didn't know what to say. "So I was a bad father," I said finally, never realizing it until that moment.

"You weren't a bad father. And like I said, I didn't understand anything about it until much later."

"Well I'm sorry I did that to you then."

"It's fine." He turned and opened the door wide to step in and look at it more closely.

"I never was able to find the piece I dropped," I said, regret filling me once again.

"I know. You weren't ever going to find it."

"Oh, how's that?"

"I found it in the morning and hid it. All these years, I've been holding on to it. You couldn't have known, but I did."

Going over to the door, where his jacket was hanging, he unzipped an inner pocket and produced the piece from within.

"All this time... you never told me?" I said. I didn't know what to feel anymore, it was all so confusing to me. My grandson wobbled in my hands and returned my attention down away from Mike. Mike was that size once. So long ago.

"I don't know why I didn't. Especially once I grew up and realized you were just so upset about it. Anyway. Not much of a peace offering, but maybe this can be a place to start."

He handed the piece to me.

Breakfast

"You have strange ideas if you think this qualifies as breakfast."

Audrey is a few steps ahead of me, barely looks over her shoulder, laughing at me. I only see her outline in the darkness of the pre-dawn morning, little specks of light glinting off the sky, water on to her form. She doesn't slow down, nor does she acknowledge my criticism. I don't blame her. I complain too much. It's something I'm working on.

The sand underfoot is in that state where half the time it is firm like regular ground, and the other half, my feet sink into the sand and threaten to trip me up as it resists me moving. Audrey is barefoot even though it is dark, even though it is too cold for bare feet, because she loves the feeling of sand underfoot too much. I'm wearing shoes because she laughs about my "baby feet" when we walk during the day, and I don't want to hurt myself on the shells and rocks on the beach. Such a difference between us; she grew up coming here, and this is still so new to me.

The rocks are up ahead. A dark line against a backdrop of darkness, only outlined by the slight brightness that starts to accumulate on the horizon. Two lights flash in the darkness, green and ominous to me. One sits out in the water on a swaying, bobbing buoy. The other at the end of the rocks, at the far end of a path of boulders piled up that tourists use to fish off of, and the boats use as protection as they come in from the greater ocean into the harbor. I know these things because Audrey's told me about them. This is still all so new, but then, it is wonderful as well. It's tough to be upset when the person bringing you has such unbridled joy about everything out here.

In fact, I only grumbled slightly about waking up so early. Mostly because she had already made me my tea, and she made it just the way I like it.

The tea is in an insulated cup in hand, half gone already, and cooling. She's got coffee in a thermos in her bag. She doesn't slow down to drink it. She's on a mission.

In my thoughts, I slowed down enough that she's already at the rocks. Or at least I assume she is, since I can only make out the memory of her in the darkness. Oh yes, there she is waving. Impatiently, I guess, but in a playful way. I wave back, and she starts to clamber up the rocks like she's been doing this all her life. She has. This is her place, and it is her place because she's been coming up here for the last thirty years. Maybe more.

I jog the rest of the way and by the time I catch up, she's already on top and looking up and down the jetty beyond. There's enough light now that it catches on her face and I can't believe how beautiful she is in that light. She turns and looks down at me.

"What are you doing? Come on! We're going to miss it."

I stumble through my words, trying to let her know I'm looking at her, while simultaneously fumbling around, and hoping I don't slip and spill my tea or scrape my knees or anything like that. Once I start up, her focus returns to the water. We'd been walking high enough on the shore that the soft murmur of the waves hitting the shore were distant. As I ascend, I hear the gurgle of the waves down the jetty, heading into the harbor.

Audrey takes my tea so I can scramble up the rest of the way and returns it to me as I get to my feet. She gives me a moment to look at the slight golden of the horizon, deepening in color, warning us that dawn is almost upon us. The boulders are dangerous in the dark, but we make our way along it, hand in hand. Tide is almost at its lowest, but still, as we get farther along the rocks, we are surrounded by water everywhere and soon all I hear is the water cozying up close to the rocks below. Sliding along, murmuring its love, and then pulling away, saying it in reverse. The sing song of the water is mesmerizing, and before I know it, we're standing under the blinking green light at the end. Further out, in the water, the other light sways and nods and blinks like an uncertain spirit, bobbing in the soft rhythm of the ocean.

Audrey picks a spot to sit, her feet dangling off the edge of a granite boulder easily ten feet to a side, or more. I am too slow to lay a blanket underneath us, but I pull it out of my bag anyway and drape it over us. The wind is light, barely pulling up the edges of the blanket, but I still tuck the corner under me so I don't need to hold onto it.

She pours out coffee into the top of her thermos, hums contentedly as she takes a sip.

Somehow we still have a few minutes until the top of the sun peeks up over the horizon, and the colors are brilliant - so many that they defy cataloging. Every time we come out here, I think I should bring a camera to capture it, but I never do. I end up settling for a few snapped pictures from my phone that never do it justice. Instead, this morning, I drink my tea, snuggle up closer to Audrey. Perfect little moment, marred only by the seagull that drips something on the rock right next to me. I hope it is just water from the ocean. I suspect it is not.

Cat Discussion

"What are those two doing up there?" Ma' remarked, standing in the front of our yard, looking up at the roof.

"What are you talking about?" I asked from the porch, standing and then joining her and trying to figure out what she was looking at. There on the roof were our two cats - Fi and Fo - laying down and being their lazy selves. Their gazes were intent on the electrical wires to the house; more specifically, the birds that were perched there some five or six meters away on the line.

"Well, I would guess they're talking about how to get them birds," I suggested. Fi looked down at me with disdain. Fi looked at everyone with disdain of course; cats did that as a matter of living, but Fi was exceptionally good at making you feel like you were both a disappointment and an intrusion at any given moment. "I think we're bothering them." I added, then returned to the porch. My sweet tea was on the table there and it was too hot a day to be far away from it. Ma' spat up at the errant cats and then joined me on the porch.

"Why on earth would they hunt?" she asked, incredulous. "We give them everything they could possibly want, don't we?"

I shook my head. "No, Ma'. Those cats are natural hunters and we don't provide them anything to hunt for. And if we did, it probably wouldn't satisfy them like hunting after live prey. That's just their nature. It is what they live for."

I had read once that cats were the only creatures in the wild who hunted without the need for food. They hunted for hunting's sake. I wasn't sure how much I believed that - all the cats I ever met were satisfied just laying on the ground until something came to them that they could hunt. Fi and Fo were the only ones I had seen who actively hunted. And even then, they often sat next to each other, conspiring more than actually hunting. I sipped my tea. It was delicious. Ma' drank from her own glass, downing most of it in one swallow. She liked her tea.

There was a scrabble of claws and noise from above us and Fi, somehow, came careening over the edge of the roof, flying out in the air toward the birds. She was far short of them, scrabbled in the air to get purchase on the wires, failed to do that, then twisted around and landed on her feet. It was an amazing sight, and if it weren't for the utter failure of it, Fi might have still looked a little triumphant. The birds on the wire though cackled like they knew what those cats were up to and were not threatened by them in the least. Fi stared them down aggressively, then stalked over to the tree and climbed back up to the roof.

"Determined, isn't she?" I said, absent-mindedly.

Ma' grunted in agreement. I looked over and saw that she had closed her eyes. Time for her nap then. Well, it was a hot day, and good for napping in the shade of the porch, especially after a refreshing glass of tea.

I watched the road, the yard, the nature around us. We lived in a rural part of town, even though the town center was built up quite a bit. Here on the outskirts, we had neighbors at a comfortable distance away, and the roads were quiet and tranquil. It was the kind of place I dreamed of living in even as a kid. And now that I had found it, I was content to stay here until my dying days. I took another sip of tea, savored the sweetness in my mouth a moment, then swallowed. I set the glass back down on the table.

There was a slight breeze out, and aside from the baking sun in the wide open, it would have been a pleasant day out in the yard I expected. I thought about giving a call over to Jim and maybe going canoeing, but that seemed like a bit of work and it would probably be hotter than I'd like out in the open water. Still, on a lazy day, it was a good distraction some times. And if Ma' was giong to be napping, it would at least keep me from accidentally waking her up at least.

There was another scrabbling on the roof and Fi came rocketing over the edge again. This jump was much better timed from what I could tell, but she still came far short of the birds. She did however catch the power lines on the way down, used them to balance and try for another jump. However, power lines are not sturdy surfaces, so when she pushed off for the second jump, she flailed out in a way she wasn't planning, and had to scramble in the air to shift around and land on her feet. Fi was not the most graceful cat, I decided, but she was persistent at least.

Even though the wires were dancing around and the cat had gotten much closer this time, the birds were not even the least bit concerned. They cackled down at Fi, mocking her in her attempts to catch them.

I had seen a cat catch a bird on the wing once, but it was because the cat was well hidden before hand. With them out on the roof like that, it seemed unlikely that the birds would just stay put while the cat grabbed them. Still, Fi was pretty innovative in how she was approaching the situation. Fo hadn't jumped out yet. I wondered if Fo was laughing at Fi just like the birds were. I hadn't heard anything from her though.

Fi was already stalking back toward the tree to climb back up to the roof, keeping her glare firmly on the birds who were now fully engaged with ridiculing the cat. Fi was furious. I was still surprised she could jump out so far.

I got up from my chair, finished off the tea, and then grabbed the chair and moved it out off of the porch and into the yard, under the shade of our tree and within sight of both the cats and the birds. Fo was still in place where she was when Ma' first saw them; Fi was just getting on the roof from the tree, dancing lightly from the branch and down onto the roof like she was calmly walking a balance beam and then dismounting casually. She settled down next to Fo, who readjusted a little as Fi was too close.

Even in the shade of the tree, it was probably another few degrees warmer than the porch; I couldn't imagine how hot it was for the cats up there in the sun. Fi wasn't going to stay long up there though, I could see her already itching to try again for the birds. She ascended the roof to the apex, then darted down, scrabbling with her claws for traction as she went, and just as she hit the corner of the roof, she leaped. Fi leaping was pure art in motion and I marveled as she flew threw the air towards the birds. She was well short of them again, but she cleared more than three meters easily, and more than half the distance easily enough. Once again, she hit the wires, and tried to use them to relaunch at the birds, but, as before, the wires swayed and sent her off at a different angle. She got more purchase on this attempt though, so she wasn't nearly as off-balance as she came to the ground. And she came to the ground without her quarry.

Out of the corner of my eye, I saw Fo move and so I turned my attention to her, expecting her to make an attempt at the birds. However, to my surprise, she came over to the tree, limberly hopped onto a limb and then climbed down the trunk. She came up onto my lap and sat down, purring. I pet her hot fur and could feel the heat radiating off of her. The shade would cool her off of course, but it was hot in the meantime with her in my lap. Luckily, I liked having cats around. Soon enough, she was asleep there, or at the least, pretending to be asleep.

Meanwhile, the bird peanut gallery was steadily mocking Fi. One bird even flew down to the ground and pecked at it to taunt Fi. She didn't take the bait though and instead returned to the tree. She glared at Fo, asleep in my lap, as if to call her a traitor. Or lazy. Or a good-for-nothing-cat. Or something similar anyway. I'm not sure I could agree with Fi though, it looked like her efforts were going to be for nothing in the end, even through her persistence.

Fi settled down on the roof for a moment, but seemed content to just sit up there this time, rather than to jump out again. I watched her as I pet at Fo, but it seemed that the hunt might be over as Fi closed her eyes while on the roof. Maybe she was going to take a nap too, and decided that there wasn't enough room on my lap. That would surprise me though - the two of them had been content on my lap before - but for now she seemed content to be on the roof anyway.

I listened again to the birds, and to the noise of a car some road away that would never pass by the house. Such a peaceful day, such a good day to just enjoy being. I didn't take many days like that these days. Work always had me occupied and when I was at home, I frequently obsessed about what needed to be done the next day. Ma' chastised me for not leaving work at work, but it was just so very difficult to do that sometimes.

The breeze blew across my yard again and I just relaxed further in it. I had a mind to bring out my hammock to lie in and take a proper nap, but it just seemed like so much effort, and with Fo asleep on my lap, it didn't seem likely to provide enough drive for me to go get it. The fact was, I probably should have been doing something more productive. Like clearing the weeds from the garden or collecting the vegetables that were ready. Or bagging the trash. Or doing the myriad other things that were always there to do but I never really wanted to do. I contemplated my cats for a moment, and was a little jealous at how they could just spend their days relaxing and lazing about as if the whole world was there to serve them. And in a way, we were. I was the one who set food out for them, got them water, changed their litter box, let them out of the house, let them back in the house. The more I thought about it, the more disappointed I was in them. They really did nothing to help. And the idle hunting of birds had only provided a little bit of entertainment. Still, I pet Fo, settled so peacefully on my lap. Like a good servant, I was just there to do as she bade. And right now, she wanted me to sit still and pet her. How did it come to this?

It was comfortable there under the tree, and now that Fo had cooled down, she was comfortable in my lap too. I settled into my chair a little, which disturbed her slightly, enough to have her reposition on my legs, and then closed her eyes once again. It was a beautiful day, and a good day for a nap. I lamented not bringing out the hammock, but maybe that was just another day waiting to happen. How often would I get such a good relaxing spot under the tree?

The answer, to my surprise, was never. Just then, Fo shot up out of her sleep, dug her claws into me and leaped off my lap in one movement, using all of her body to propel herself forward. She was a blur across the yard, and over to the spot below the birds, where she did a vertical leap, defying all of gravity and physics, up to where the birds were and nabbed one right off the wire before it could even react. The other birds flew up and away in slow motion as the one in Fo's mouth struggled desperately. She landed down on the ground, regally, proud, and then ended that poor bird's life in a single stroke.

Meanwhile, my legs were on fire with pain from her claws digging in to me, but it was hard for me to concentrate on that when I had witnessed such an amazing act of grace and violence all at once. Never would I see a cat perform such acrobatics again in my life. It was as if Fo needed to show up Fi just the one time. As the elder cat, it was her place to remind Fi just how much she didn't know. Fo walked triumphantly, and nonchalantly back over under the tree, considered my lap for a moment and looked at me.

"You are not bringing that bird up into my lap, Fo." I was a little disgusted at the brutal act I witnessed, and I certainly didn't want a dead bird to settle in on my lap with the cat. Fo seemed to get the message and meandered off with the bird, no doubt looking for a quiet place to play with her kill. Fi, still up on the roof, was now standing at the roof's edge, watching Fo move about like a jealous lover. Fo paid her no heed and walked off to her own hidden spot.

The pain in my legs was coming more to my attention now that the excitement was over and I saw that Fo had not only pierced the skin in a few spots, but also ripped my pants in the process. It was amazing to me she was able to build such momentum in one jump, but cats were like tightly wound springs. They could leap at nothing, or, like now, they could leap with a purpose all to themselves. In this case, leaping to show the other cat who was boss in the house. Something told me that Fi would not be getting in Fo's way any time soon. I wasn't sure I wanted to either.

I dragged my chair back to the porch and set it down. Now that the excitement was over, I supposed it was time to think about what to make for dinner anyway. Nothing with chicken, that was for sure. Brussel sprouts? That sounded good to me anyway.

"Hey, Ma' - you going to sleep out there all night?" I called out through the open window. She stirred, and would join me eventually. First, she needed to catch her bearings. One thing was for sure, cats had a leg up on us humans. They could sleep as soundly as anything, but could also be awake in a moment's call, without any drowsiness if the need called for it. Another thing to admire about them I supposed.

I took care of my war wounds, changed my pants and left them out so that I could mend them later, and then set about making the dinner. Dark settled in some time later and there was a scratch at the door. No doubt Fo ready to come in after taking care of her own meal. However, it was Fi instead. She strolled in like a dejected lover, wandered into the kitchen and pawed at her bowl. Her bowl was empty, she was telling me. Of course, she didn't get a second meal in her day, so I had some sympathy about it. Then again, at least I wouldn't need to feed Fo too. I settled down some food in the bowl for her, and returned to the dinner preparation.

Another scratching at the door. There would be Fo now. I checked her first, to make sure she wasn't bringing in any of the bird's remnants, but she was clean of them. She was non-plussed that I would even bother to stop her for such a pedestrian thing, but when I opened the door fully, she brushed up against my legs affectionately. That was her form of apology of course. She couldn't give me the dead bird, so she rubbed up against me instead. Seemed reasonable to me. And much more preferable for that matter.

About the Author

David is a father, writer, streamer.

With the support of his partner and children, David has been creating stories daily since late 2021. "Wraith and Specter" appeared in Future's Lens (Jan 2023) and "Escape and Transform" appeared in Reality's Lens (May 2023). "Tapping at the Door" appeared in Adventures Issue 8 (Sept 2023). Most recently, "Invasive Species" appeared in Warped Lens (Sept 2023).

On stream (twitch.tv/telinartho), he writes each day both for accountability and inspiration for others.

Links:

telinartho.wordpress.com

Twitch.tv/telinartho

Mas.to/@telinartho

Bsky.app/profile/telinartho.bsky.social

Twitter.com/telinartho

Facebook.com/TelinArtho

www.ingramcontent.com/pod-product-compliance
Lightning Source LLC
Chambersburg PA
CBHW022052150726
47990CB00003B/1063